W9-BPO-703

A NOTE TO PARENTS

When your children are ready to "step into reading," giving them the right books—and lots of them—is as crucial as giving them the right food to eat. **Step into Reading Books** present exciting stories and information reinforced with lively, colorful illustrations that make learning to read fun, satisfying, and worthwhile. They are priced so that acquiring an entire library of them is affordable. And they are beginning readers with an important difference—they're written on four levels.

Step 1 Books, with their very large type and extremely simple vocabulary, have been created for the very youngest readers. **Step 2 Books** are both longer and slightly more difficult. **Step 3 Books,** written to mid-second-grade reading levels, are for the child who has acquired even greater reading skills. **Step 4 Books** offer exciting nonfiction for the increasingly proficient reader.

Children develop at different ages. **Step into Reading Books,** with their four levels of reading, are designed to help children become good—and interested—readers *faster.* The grade levels assigned to the four steps—preschool through grade 1 for Step 1, grades 1 through 3 for Step 2, grades 2 and 3 for Step 3, and grades 2 through 4 for Step 4—are intended only as guides. Some children move through all four steps very rapidly; others climb the steps over a period of several years. These books will help your child "step into reading" in style!

Text copyright © 1984, 1993 by Random House, Inc. Illustrations copyright © 1993 by Thomas La Padula. All rights reserved under International and Pan-American Copyright Conventions. Published in the United States by Random House, Inc., New York, and simultaneously in Canada by Random House of Canada Limited, Toronto. This is an abridged edition of a work originally published by Random House, Inc., in 1984.

Library of Congress Cataloging-in-Publication Data
Donnelly, Judy.
True-life treasure hunts / by Judy Donnelly ; illustrated by Thomas La Padula.
    p.   cm. — (Step into reading. A Step 4 book)
SUMMARY: Describes several successful searches for lost treasure, including discoveries of sunken Spanish ships off the coast of Florida, the sacred well of the Mayans in Yucatan, and the Lost Dutchman Mine in Arizona.
ISBN 0-679-83980-1 (pbk.)—ISBN 0-679-93980-6 (lib. bdg.)
1. Treasure-trove—Juvenile literature.   [1. Buried treasure.   2. Archaeology.]
I. LaPadula, Tom, ill.   II. Title.   III. Series: Step into reading. Step 4 book.
G525.D59   1993   930.1—dc20   93-20203

Manufactured in the United States of America   10 9 8 7

Step into Reading

TRUE-LIFE TREASURE HUNTS

By Judy Donnelly

Illustrated by Thomas La Padula

A Step 4 Book

Random House 🏠 New York

Pirate Gold

Just imagine . . .

It is midnight on a lonely island. Two men are digging on the sandy shore. One wears a gold earring and a red bandanna. The other man has a patch over his eye. Both are armed with swords and guns. They are pirates.

Slowly they lower a heavy wooden chest into a deep hole. The chest is heavy because it is full of gold and jewels. The pirates shovel sand into the hole. After they are finished, no one would guess that treasure is buried in this place. The pirates leave quickly.

They never return.

Is this a true story? Maybe. Treasure hunters are sure that pirates buried stolen gold in secret places all over the world. And they believe that lots of pirate treasure is still waiting for someone to discover it.

Pirates sailed the seas hundreds of years ago. They attacked ships with rich cargoes—ships full of gold and jewels. They took everything they wanted. Pirates didn't get any regular pay. Each man got a share of what was stolen from the captured ship. So the more treasure on board the better.

Pirates were always ready for a fight. But they liked it better if sailors gave up without a battle. So they tried to scare them. Pirates flew a flag called the Jolly Roger. It wasn't jolly. It was usually black with a white skull on it. Usually there were crossbones beneath the skull. Sometimes it had an hourglass on it too. That meant "Your time is running out!"

One pirate scared everybody—even other pirates. He was a giant of a man. He had wild eyes. He wore six guns, two sharp curved swords, and two or three daggers. His real name was Edward Teach or Thatch—nobody knows for sure. But everybody called him Blackbeard. He liked to tie red ribbons in his long, scraggly beard. One time he even tied burning candles in it. But the whole thing caught fire. He never did that again!

Blackbeard was as scary as he looked. Once, for no reason at all, he shot a friend. Blackbeard explained it this way: "If I don't shoot somebody now and then, people will forget who I am."

Blackbeard sailed the seas in the early 1700s. He attacked ships up and down the coast of North America. He is said to have buried lots of treasure. The stories usually add that he buried a headless skeleton along with his gold. Some people say that Blackbeard hid his loot on the Isles of Shoals, off the coast of New Hampshire. Others say he buried it off the coast of North Carolina or Georgia. But nothing much has been found. Blackbeard didn't leave many clues. He always said, "Only the Devil and me knows where my gold is hid."

There are many other stories of pirate treasure. Cocos Island, off Central America, has even been nicknamed "Treasure Island." Has treasure been found there? No. But almost 500 separate groups of people have gone to Cocos to look for treasure! Why so many? Because stories say that four or five different pirates buried gold somewhere on the island.

Many pirates really did visit one special island. But not to hide their gold. To spend it.

They went to the town of Port Royal on the island of Jamaica. In the 1600s, Port Royal was called "the wickedest city in the world." Pirates from all over met there. They came in their fanciest clothes—leather boots, bright silk sashes, gold bracelets, and armbands. They came to gamble. They came to fight. They came to get drunk on one of their favorite drinks—rum and gunpowder.

Then, in just a few minutes, Port Royal changed forever. It happened on the morning of June 7, 1692. Suddenly, houses began to shake. People ran outside crying "Earthquake!" The streets started to rise like waves in the sea. Great cracks opened in the ground. Men and women were swallowed up. Buildings crumbled and fell. Then a huge wave, taller than the tallest building, swept over Port Royal. Most of the city and 2,000 people slid to the bottom of the sea.

An old print of the earthquake at Port Royal.

Many years passed. People told strange stories about the lost city. They said there were rows of buildings standing on the sea bottom. Sunken streets paved with gold. Underwater taverns with

11

skeletons sitting at the tables. And pirate treasure everywhere.

The stories weren't true. But many divers believed them. They tried to swim down to the sunken city. All they found was mud. The city was buried.

Then, in 1965, a famous diver came to Port Royal. His name was Robert Marx. He brought men and machines with him. He wanted to explore the sunken city and find out how life had been lived there.

His work was dangerous. There were sharks and stinging fish in the water. Once a huge winged fish called a manta ray swam by. It was 12 feet wide! It put its great wings around one diver. It hugged him. Then it swam off!

Soon Marx found the walls of the city. He brought up clay smoking pipes, candlesticks, old rum bottles, a silver watch, and much more. He even found two buildings still standing. He was happy

to discover so many clues about life in old Port Royal. Marx wasn't really looking for treasure. But he found it! He and his divers were exploring near the ruins of an old tavern. They found a few silver coins. Then thousands of them. Treasure from the pirate city!

Treasure hunters were thrilled at the news. Many others came to search the ruins of Port Royal. But many more kept on exploring lonely little islands where nothing had been found yet. They still felt sure that somewhere, in a wooden chest, buried in a sandy beach, pirate gold was waiting.

Sunken Treasure

July 30, 1715. Eleven ships sailed slowly along the coast of Florida. They were heavy with silver and gold. About 2,000 sailors were on board. The ships had to take their treasure all the way back to Spain—about 5,000 miles away. The voyage would be full of danger. Pirates sailed the ocean. Hurricanes struck without warning. And the sea was full of reefs—hard, jagged ridges hidden just underwater. If the bottom of a ship scraped against one, it would be torn open.

The sea was very still. The ships were barely moving. Then the sky grew dark. Rain began to fall. The winds howled and giant waves crashed down. The storm grew worse. Now the waves were like mountains. Men were swept overboard. Wood cracked. Sails tore. Tons of water poured down. The ships were pushed toward the reefs. One ship sank to the bottom. Then another and another.

Ten ships went down in the terrible storm. A thousand men died. A fortune in treasure was lost.

Almost 250 years later a man was walking along a Florida beach. His name was Kip Wagner. His job was building houses. He had moved to a nearby town to build a new motel.

Kip was looking for old silver coins. He had been looking for years. He had heard stories about Spanish coins turning up on the beach—pieces of eight that came from sunken treasure ships. When a friend finally showed him some pieces of eight, Kip was surprised. They weren't round. They weren't shiny. They weren't anything like the coins in his pocket. They were oddly shaped and blackened by the sea. If he had seen one, he would never have bothered to pick it up.

Even knowing what to look for didn't help Kip. He never found anything. Sometimes he thought he never would.

Kip used a metal detector. He would sweep the rod back and forth over the beach. If there was any metal under the sand, the detector would make a special noise. A beep.

Often the metal detector beeped. Kip would dig in the sand. And what would he find? A tin can.

Then one day the detector beeped the way it always did. Kip brushed away the sand. This time he saw a black, strangely shaped piece of metal. He couldn't believe it! An old silver coin! He had finally found one!

Kip picked it up. Pirates had killed for these coins. Treasure hunters had died trying to find them. And now he held one in his hand.

Kip decided something. He would never give up searching until he found a great treasure.

Kip went back to the same beach again

and again. He found more silver coins, even some gold ones. He began to call the place his "money beach."

He had one big question. Where had all these coins come from? He felt sure they had washed up from the sea. Somewhere, probably nearby, was the wreck of a great treasure ship.

Kip swam out to look for the wreck. He cut himself on the sharp edges of the reefs. But he found nothing. He borrowed a boat. He cruised through the waves. He stared down into the water. Still nothing.

He was never going to find any treasure this way. He had to know where to look. He decided to stop searching in the ocean. Instead, he would search for answers in the library!

Kip had one important clue. The coins from the beach had dates on them. And no coin was dated later than 1715. He heard that some treasure ships had gone down

in a hurricane in 1715. But no one knew where they had sunk.

Kip tried the biggest library in the country. The Library of Congress, in Washington, D.C. The library had a very rare book. It was 200 years old. Sure enough, it told about the shipwrecks of 1715! There was even a map! The map showed that the treasure ships had gone down within a few miles of his money beach!

Kip took to the ocean again. This time he made himself a special surfboard. He put a glass window in it. He could paddle along and see down into the water. Time after time Kip went out looking for a wrecked ship beneath the waves.

Then one day he saw strange shapes. He paddled closer. They were cannons from a ship. Nearby was a huge anchor. Suddenly he knew. He had found the wreck! He had expected to see a whole ship lying on its side. But a wooden ship would be rotted away after almost 250 years in the ocean. Only the metal parts would last.

And the treasure? Kip was sure it was still there. But it must be scattered and buried under the sand.

Kip got special permission from the Florida government to search for treasure. He promised to give Florida part of any treasure he found. He bought an old boat and machines to move sand. He spent a year getting a team of eight men together. He liked and trusted every one of them. One morning, in January 1961, he set out for the wreck.

The team was excited. Kip was nervous. Storms made the sand at the bottom of the ocean move. What you could see one day might be covered up the next. Would he be able to find the wreck again?

The sea was rough. Kip had to

steer the boat close to two dangerous reefs—the same reefs that had sunk the treasure ships.

The boat made it. The water was very cold. Only two of the team had special diving suits to keep them warm. Down they went.

Then one diver broke through the water. He waved a handful of silver coins. "They're down there by the bushel!" he cried. He left the coins on the deck and disappeared. Then he was back, pushing what looked like a big black rock onto the ship. It was a mass of silver coins—all stuck together. There had to be a thousand of them!

Everyone began to laugh and shout "We're rich! We're rich!" And they all dived in! Nobody cared how cold the water was! For the rest of the day they picked treasure off the bottom—some $80,000 worth.

And this was only the beginning. Later they found gold coins, jewelry, silver candlesticks. Their discoveries surprised the world. They found a gold chain 10½ feet long! They found a wooden treasure chest. It was loaded with 3,000 coins. How had a wooden chest survived 250 years in the sea? No one could believe it. They found something even stranger—28 priceless cups and saucers from China. Not one was even cracked.

That wasn't all. Kip led his team to seven more treasure wrecks! They found more than $3 million in treasure!

Kip had made his dream come true. He was famous. Reporters followed him. He was invited all over the world. He was on television, in magazines. Treasure hunters everywhere tried to do what he had done.

And this was the man who thought he would never find even one silver coin!

The Sacred Well

Deep in the jungles of Mexico stands an empty city. It is called Chichén Itzá (chee-CHEN eat-SAH). It was built more than a thousand years ago by the Mayan Indians. The Mayan empire spread over parts of Mexico and Central America. The Mayans built many beautiful cities. But they deserted them. No one is sure why.

In 1904 a man named Edward Thompson was walking in the empty city of Chichén Itzá. He had come to learn about the Mayan people.

He followed a path that led to a mysterious pool of water. It was called the Sacred Well. It was as big as a small lake—almost 200 feet wide. Its water was strange and dark and still. It was very, very deep.

The Indians who lived in the jungle were afraid of the well. They said giant snakes and monsters lived at the bottom. They said sometimes the water turned to blood. And indeed Edward noticed that the water often did change to a dark reddish color.

Once Edward had read a strange old story. It said the Mayans believed a rain god lived in the bottom of the well. Sometimes rain didn't fall. Sometimes crops didn't grow. The Mayans thought the rain god was angry then. So they would march slowly to the well. They would throw rich treasure and beautiful young girls into the dark water. The Mayans hoped their actions would please the rain god.

Edward could not forget this story. He wanted to explore the mysterious well.

His family and friends thought he was crazy. They tried to make him change his mind. But Edward went ahead anyway.

He took deep-sea diving lessons. Then he bought a machine called a dredge. The machine had a bucket that hung from a long steel rope. Edward could lower the bucket into the well. It could scoop up whatever was at the bottom and bring it up.

But where should he dig? The well was so big. Then he remembered the story about treasure and girls thrown into the well. He found logs the size and shape of a human being. One by one he threw them into the dark water. They all fell in at about the same spot. That was where the young girls must have fallen, too. That was the place to lower the dredge.

Day after day Edward and his Indian helpers worked at the well. But the dredge brought up only sticks and mud.

Weeks passed. One day, just as usual, the dredge came up with sticks and mud. But hidden in the mud was treasure!

Each day there was more. A golden bowl and cups. A bell. Beautiful necklaces. Rings that had been worn a thousand years before.

Treasure *had* been thrown into the Sacred Well! But was the rest of the story true? Edward soon knew the answer.

The dredge found human skeletons.

But Edward wasn't satisfied. The dredge was coming up empty again. It had hit bottom. He decided to dive into the well and explore its hidden places.

Again his friends tried to get Edward to change his mind. They said, "No one can go down into the well and come out alive!"

But Edward did not listen. He climbed into his diving suit. It had a big helmet, a long air hose, and iron shoes. The heavy shoes would drag him down to the bottom of the well. His Indian helpers would pump down air for him to breathe. They had to do their job carefully. Edward's life depended on them.

One by one his helpers shook his hand. Their faces were sad. They thought they would never see him again.

When Edward jumped into the well, he sank down, down, down. He felt pain in his ears. The water was so dark, he couldn't see at all.

At last his iron shoes touched bottom. He felt a strange thrill. So many people had died in this place. But *he* was going to come out alive!

He turned on his flashlight. It didn't help. Here the water was like thick mud soup. He had to feel his way. But Edward got used to the strange darkness. And he went down into the well again and again. In the deepest part he came upon the skeletons of three women. They looked as though they were reaching out for help. One still wore a necklace.

Edward found many skeletons in the well. Skeletons of women, men, and children, too. Some were probably slaves. Some may have been prisoners of the Mayans. Edward was sure they had died because the Mayans were trying to please the rain god.

Edward found much more treasure too. Weapons and jewelry. Strange carvings. Even scraps of clothing. He hoped these things would help scientists learn more about the ancient Mayans.

Edward kept working at the well. Finally he went home to the United States. He was a hero. He had risked his life. And he had solved a mystery—the mystery of the Sacred Well.

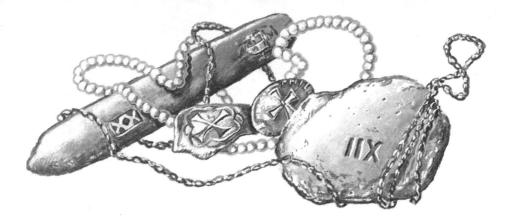

Treasure, Treasure Everywhere

How much treasure is still lost or buried? Billions of dollars' worth. In gold and silver and jewels! Treasure hunters all agree on this. Why so much? People have been hiding and losing treasure for thousands of years. It adds up!

Here are some famous stories about lost treasures still waiting to be found.

Sunken Treasure

Some of the biggest treasures are underwater. Hundreds of ships full of gold lie on the ocean bottom. There are treasure ships in lakes and rivers, too. One sunken

treasure ship is in a very surprising place. It's on the bottom of one of the world's busiest harbors. Right off East 135th Street in New York City! And it's been there since 1780! The ship's name is the

Hussar. It was sent from England with $2 million in silver and gold. The money was meant to pay British soldiers in America. The *Hussar*'s anchor has been found. But no one has brought up the gold.

It sounds as if it would be so easy to get the treasure. But it is not. The *Hussar* went down in deep water. At the time the ship sank, treasure hunters didn't have inventions like diving suits to help them search the bottom. Today there are other problems. The ship has been underwater for over 200 years. So the wreck has probably rotted away. And the river bottom is made up of at least 15 feet of soft ooze and trash. By now, experts say, the gold may be scattered along miles of the river. And buried in that ooze.

Even if nobody ever finds the *Hussar,* there are plenty of other ships to look for. There are stories of sunken treasure ships from all over the world. People say that there's a steamboat at the bottom of the Mississippi River. It sank in 1871 with a fortune on board. There are treasure wrecks as far away as Japan and Australia. There's even a sunken treasure *train*! In 1876 the train plunged into a river in Ohio. One car held $2 million in gold bars.

Pirate Treasure

There were a lot of other famous pirates besides Blackbeard. Many are said to have buried treasure.

Sometimes when pirates were caught, they told where the buried treasure was. Once there was a pirate named Charles Wilson. Right before he was hanged, he gave directions to his treasure. He named an island in Maryland and said, "Ye treasure lies hidden in a clump of trees near three creeks lying a hundred paces or more north of the second inlet." People rushed to the island. But no one found the treasure.

Stolen Goods

Lots of treasure gets stolen. And there's a funny thing about robbers. They're scared of other robbers! So they often hide what they steal. Many outlaws of the Old West hid their loot. Jesse James

is one of the most famous. He robbed
stagecoaches, trains, and banks during
the 1870s. But he was polite. He liked to
pause when he was robbing somebody and
introduce his gang members. Once the
James Gang stole a million dollars in
gold bars. People say Jesse buried it near

Lawton, Oklahoma. He marked the spot with two ax heads and a bucket. But before he could go back for it, he was killed. As far as anybody knows, the treasure is still there. Somewhere.

Hidden Tombs

Many people buried their dead with treasure. Hidden tombs full of gold and jewels have been found all over the world. The biggest tomb was found in China. It just looked like a big grassy hill covered with trees. But in 1974 some men started to dig a well. And they found the burial place of an emperor! The tomb went on for miles. It was over 2,000 years old. Inside was treasure—and an army of thousands of life-size clay people, horses, and chariots. Archaeologists believe that many other hidden tombs are yet to be found—tombs of kings and queens and nobles buried long, long ago.

War Loot

Lots of people hide treasure in wartime so that the enemy can't take it. Sometimes they get killed. Sometimes they forget where the treasure is. So the treasure stays where it was hidden.

Lots of treasure gets stolen in wartime too. During World War II, Hitler and his men stole gold and jewels and paintings and statues from many countries. After the fighting was over, people tried to find Hitler's stolen treasure. And they did! It was hidden in secret caves, old mines, and castles all over Germany. But did they find it all? Many treasure hunters say no. It's still there waiting to be found.

Lost Mines

How do you lose a gold mine? It must be easy, because treasure hunters tell lots of stories about gold mines that were found and then lost.

One famous story is about the Lost Breyfogle Mine. It is named for the man who found it and lost it—Jacob Breyfogle. Around 1865 he was trying to cross a desert in California called Death Valley. His horse died. He ran out of food and water. He had to live on bugs, roots, and herbs. But he kept going. Suddenly he saw a rich vein of gold and silver in some pink rocks. He took all he could fit in his pack. He carried it until he finally made it to a town. Then he tried to go back to the place that would make him rich. It was no use. He never did find the spot. But every year treasure hunters go to Death Valley to try their luck.

Then there's the Lost Dutchman Mine. The story goes like this. In the 1870s a man called the Dutchman found gold in the Arizona mountains. He brought out sacks of nuggets. He bragged about his mine. But he wouldn't tell anyone where it was. Different men tried to trail him. None were seen again. After the Dutch-man died, thousands more people tried to find the mine. A few of them were found murdered. It is said there's an Indian curse on the mine. Or that an old miner shoots anyone who comes near. One thing is sure. The Lost Dutchman Mine is still lost.

Treasure, Treasure Anywhere

Treasure may be hidden anywhere. On a mountaintop. In a swamp. Even in the middle of a busy city. Once a woman moved into a new apartment in New York City. She defrosted her refriger-ator. When the ice melted, she found a dozen thousand-dollar bills taped inside the freezer! In 1926 two teenagers were plowing a field in Tennessee. A gold coin gleamed in the soil. And another. Soon they had a whole jar full!

Nobody was even looking for these treasures. Nobody told any stories about them. They were a big surprise! And sometime, maybe even today, someone will find another hidden treasure. It could be a pirate chest. Or a king's crown. Or a strange, wonderful treasure like nothing that has ever been discovered before. Who can tell? There are so many hidden treasures to find!